A FIGHT TO THE FINISH!

Will stood squarely in the lane, blocking Brian's path to the hoop. Brian slowed and turned around, keeping his back to the basket. He edged a little closer, then bobbed his head once. It was just enough to bring Will to his toes—giving Brian the split second he needed to outjump him.

Brian pushed off with his feet and spun. His fadeaway jumper barely cleared the top of Will's fingertips.

Swish.

"Now who's getting burned?" he whispered under his breath.

Faking Will out had felt good. But the game was still only tied at two baskets each. The grudge match had barely started.

Brian wiped his forehead. It was going to be a *long* afternoon.

TRASH TALK

by
Hank Herman

BANTAM BOOKS
NEW YORK · TORONTO · LONDON · SYDNEY · AUCKLAND

RL 2.6, 007-010

TRASH TALK
A Bantam Book / March 1996

Produced by Daniel Weiss Associates, Inc.
33 West 17th Street
New York, NY 10011

Cover art by Jeff Mangiat

All rights reserved.

Copyright © 1996 by Daniel Weiss Associates, Inc., and
Daniel Ehrenhaft.

ISBN: 0-553-48275-0
Published simultaneously in the United States and Canada

Bantam Books are published by Bantam Books, a division of Bantam
Doubleday Dell Publishing Group, Inc. Its trademark, consisting of the
words "Bantam Books" and the portrayal of a rooster, is Registered in U.S.
Patent and Trademark Office and in other countries. Marca Registrada.
Bantam Books, 1540 Broadway, New York, New York 10036.

PRINTED IN THE UNITED STATES OF AMERICA

OPM   0 9 8 7 6 5 4 3 2

"Do something with the ball, Will!" shouted a voice from the sidelines. "Pass or shoot!"

Will Hopwood was hunched over the ball inside the lane. He had his back to the basket. David Danzig was guarding him closely, glued to his every move.

Even though Will was taller than Dave, he knew he had to be careful. Dave could easily jump high enough to block a shot—and he was quick enough to steal the ball if Will didn't protect it.

He was going to have to fake Dave out.

"Come on, Will!" the voice shouted again over the blacktop at Jefferson Park, where the Bulls always practiced since their town didn't have a community center. "You've been in the lane for at least five seconds. A ref would have already nailed you for a three second violation. *Move!*"

Uh-oh, Will thought. He knew the voice well. It belonged to his sixteen-year-old brother, Jim. And when the Branford Bulls were practicing, Jim was more than Will's big brother. He was also one of Will's coaches.

"*Now!*" Jim yelled.

Suddenly Will turned on his right foot and spun toward the basket. Dave leapt up to block the shot. At the last second, Will dished an underhand pass to Brian Simmons, who had sped past Derek Roberts to get open just outside the lane. As Dave and Will came down, Brian went up for a fadeaway jump shot.

"Now *that* was pretty!" called Nate Bowman, the Bulls' other coach. Nate was a flashy seventeen-year-old with a gold hoop earring and mammoth size-13 sneakers. He was probably the best basketball player in Danville County.

"Nothing to it," Brian said.

"Well, I guess that's why they call you Fadeaway," Nate replied.

Will grinned. Nate and his father had nicknames for almost everyone. They called Brian "Fadeaway" partly because of Brian's short fade haircut—but mostly because Brian hardly ever missed his favorite shot: the fadeaway jumper.

Nate turned to Will. "Nice pass, Too-Tall."

"Thanks," Will said modestly. Will had been called "Too-Tall" since last summer—after he had grown four inches in six months.

"That's the kind of play that'll take the Bulls to the championship," Nate added. "Good, solid teamwork."

Nate has that right, Will thought as he grabbed the ball and took one last shot.

After all, teamwork was nothing new to Will. He had been playing hoops with Brian and Dave since kindergarten. As far as Will was concerned, their teamwork was what made the Branford Bulls unstoppable.

"Yo, Will, I noticed you were moving a little slow out on the court today," Dave said. He picked up the ball and began whirling it on his finger. "Your mom forget to give you your vitamins or something?"

Will rolled his eyes. Dave loved talking trash almost as much as he loved showing off.

"Well, he did move fast enough to burn *you*, Droopy," Nate said, winking at Will. "Or maybe you just couldn't see him with all that hair hanging in your eyes."

Whenever Dave made a wisecrack, Nate was always quick with a comeback—usually having something to do with Dave's "droopy" blond hair.

Dave brushed his long bangs out of his face and shrugged. "I've got to let them burn me sometimes, Coach. I just want to give the rest of these chumps a chance at sharing some of the glory. But if you want to talk bad haircuts—"

"Hey, wait a sec," Jim interrupted. "Before the trash talk gets too out of hand here, Nate and I have an important announcement to make."

"You do? What is it?" Will was surprised. Jim hadn't mentioned anything about an announcement at home.

"Uh—do you think you can tell us at Bowman's?" Chunky Schwartz asked quickly, wiping sweat off his pale forehead with a pudgy arm. "I'm pretty beat. . . ."

"Yeah, me too," Jo Meyerson chimed in. She loosened the scrunchie on her ponytail. "Let's blow this taco stand, man."

Will laughed silently to himself. Jo Meyerson always said what was on her mind. *Always*. In fact, she could trash talk better than most guys Will knew.

That was because she was Otto Meyerson's younger sister. Otto and the rest of his teammates on the Sampton Slashers had by far the meanest, ugliest, most foul mouths of any team in the Danville County Summer League.

The Slashers were the Bulls' archrivals—the team that gave them the toughest competition.

When Jo had first tried out for the Bulls, Dave hadn't been sure that a girl—especially Otto's sister—should be allowed to play. Will smiled, remembering the vicious trash talk that had exploded between Jo and Dave. But they had worked it out, and now Jo was as much a Bull as any of them.

Jim frowned. "Jo, this is important."

"But we've been practicing for three hours," Brian complained. "You know I don't like to be disrespectful, Coach, but I'm about to die of thirst."

Jim raised an eyebrow. "Brian, you saying that you don't like to be disrespectful is like Shaq saying he doesn't like to slam-dunk."

Nate chuckled. "Well, we wouldn't want Fadeaway drying up on us, now would we? Maybe I could even convince my dad to give us a few Cokes on the house today."

Will nodded eagerly. Nate's dad—Nate

Bowman, Sr.—owned Bowman's Market, which was right across the street from Jefferson Park. Ever since Will had been on the Bulls, the team had ended almost every practice at Bowman's.

"Now you're talking," said Mark Fisher, wiping his thick goggles on his shirt. "Free soda always tastes better."

Derek nodded silently, adjusting the red, white, and blue wristbands he always wore.

Will glanced at Derek. For some reason, the skinny, somber African American kid hardly ever said a word. But Derek didn't need to talk—his playing spoke for him. He was the best ten-year-old ballplayer Will had ever seen.

Will grabbed the ball from Dave and began heading off the court. "Let's go!"

"Hold on a sec, guys," Jim said. "I mean it. I just want to tell you what's up before we leave." He paused and looked around. "Nate and I are going to camp for a couple of weeks."

"What!" Will stopped dead in his tracks.

He couldn't believe what he was hearing. Earlier this summer, Jim had mentioned something about basketball camp, but there hadn't been any more available spaces. "I thought you said—" Will began.

"I found out today that they had two extra spots," Jim explained. "You had already left the house."

Will paced nervously. "I can't believe it!"

Nate started laughing. "Hey, it's cool, Too-Tall. You've got nothing to worry about. We aren't leaving you high and dry like Coach McBane did. We've taken care of everything."

Will wasn't sure. The Bulls had almost fallen apart at the beginning of the season when their old coach, Mr. McBane, had suddenly moved away. For a while it had looked like the Branford Bulls were finished—until Nate and Jim had offered to take over.

Now it sounded like the same thing was happening all over again. Finding a new coach after Coach McBane left had been tough. But who could replace Nate and Jim?

CHAPTER 2

"Another tough workout comes to an end." Nate's father poked his head out the door as the Bulls all collapsed on the bench in front of Bowman's Market. "You haven't been working these boys *too* hard, have you, son?" he asked, glancing at Nate.

"Nothing they can't handle," Nate replied.

Will had known Mr. Bowman for as long as he had known Nate. Nate's dad was a chubby, balding African

9

American man in his mid-fifties. He and his son were a lot alike. They both had the same wide smile, they both loved hoops—and they both had nicknames for everyone.

"How about some cold drinks, folks?" Mr. Bowman asked.

While Mr. Bowman was inside getting the sodas, Will turned to Jim. "So what *are* we going to do while you two are gone?"

"The same things you always do," Jim replied. "You guys will just have to run practices on your own. You'll come to Jefferson at the usual time every afternoon, and work on the things we've been talking about. Crashing the boards, passing, and outside shooting."

"You have only one game while we're gone," Nate added. "It's against Winsted."

Mr. Bowman came back outside and handed out sodas to everyone. "And I'm going to drive you guys to and from the game in my van. So everything's been taken care of. Except beating Winsted, that is."

"That shouldn't be a problem," Dave

bragged. "We don't need coaches to beat Winsted. We may not even need a basketball team."

"That's what I like to hear, Droopy," Mr. Bowman said as he started to head back inside. "Good old-fashioned trash talk."

Will heaved a sigh of relief. Winsted *was* one of the worst teams in the league.

"Aren't you guys a little *old* to be going to camp?" Jo asked with a smirk.

Dave laughed. "Yeah, what are you guys going to do—arts and crafts?"

"Droopy, don't even start," Nate said, rolling his eyes. "I don't think they do much finger-painting at *basketball* camp."

"Basketball camp!" Dave exclaimed.

"That's right." Nate grinned. "Some of the other guys from our high school are going to be there, too. Rumor has it that a couple of players from the NBA might be there as well." Nate thrust out his chest. "Although I can't imagine that they'd have anything to teach *me*. Everyone knows I'm the man."

Brian shook his head. "Maybe they'll give you some ice for your swollen head."

Nate smiled. "Fadeaway, some day when you're much older, you're going to be bragging to all your friends, 'I was coached by *the* Nate Bowman.' And if I'm feeling real generous, maybe I'll even give you an autograph to prove it."

"You know what, guys?" Brian said, turning to the rest of the Bulls. "I think this is going to be a good couple of weeks."

Jim grinned. "I figured you might say that, Brian. You never liked being coached, anyway." He looked at his watch. "Wow—it's almost seven. I've got to split. Will, I'll see you at home. I'll see the rest of you in exactly two weeks. Have fun, work hard, and beat Winsted."

As Jim turned and left, there was a knock on the inside of the store window. Mr. Bowman waved for Nate to come in. Nate made a face. "Man, the sweetest thing about going to basketball camp is that I won't have to help my dad close this place up every night." He opened the front door. "All right, guys, I'll see you later. You heard what Jim said—have fun, work hard, and beat Winsted."

Nate closed the door behind him.

Will leaned back on the bench and let the news sink in. Maybe it wasn't such a bad thing that Nate and Jim were going away, after all. Lots of times during practice, Will had wondered if he could do as good a job of coaching as Jim did.

Now he had a chance to find out.

Suddenly Will was psyched. He sat forward on the bench and grinned. "This is going to be great!" he said excitedly. "We're going to get a lot done."

Brian raised his eyebrows. "Yeah, we *could* get a lot done. But let's not go overboard. I mean, it's not every day a team gets to coach itself." He rubbed his hands together and chuckled mischievously. "We should have a little fun. Know what I'm saying?"

"Well, yeah, of course," Will said distractedly. "But I'm going to make sure we work on things that Jim and Nate don't do that much, like fancy dribbling and defensive strategies and posting up. . . ."

Will noticed that Brian's smile had turned into a frown.

Brian pointed at Will. *"You're* going to make sure we work on that stuff?"

"Why not?" Will demanded. "It'll be good for us."

"What if we don't want to work on defensive strategies?" Brian asked with a smile. "What if we only want to practice left-handed hookshots from mid-court?"

Everyone on the bench laughed.

"Come on, Brian." Will sighed. "Seriously. Jim and Nate make us work really hard. But that's why we're such a good team."

"True," Brian said. "But there's one difference. Jim and Nate are the coaches of this team. And I don't remember them saying anything about leaving *you* in charge."

Will opened his mouth, but he couldn't think of anything to say. Brian was right: neither Jim nor Nate had specifically chosen Will to coach the Bulls while they were gone. But why shouldn't he be in charge? He was Jim's brother—not to mention the best all-around player on the team besides Derek. He had figured the rest of the Bulls would think the same thing.

"They only said we had to coach ourselves," Brian went on. "That doesn't mean you're in charge. Don't you think we should check to see if anyone else wants to coach, too?"

"Fine." Will sighed. "Anybody else want to coach?"

The rest of the Bulls were silent.

"Well, *I* want to coach some of the time," Brian said. "So let's split the job. I can run half the practices—and you can run the other half."

"That sounds fair," Dave put in.

Will looked at the ground. "Okay," he said finally.

Maybe it was fair, but Will didn't like the sound of it.

CHAPTER 3

"All right, people, let's get started," Brian yelled. "First let's have a roll call. You poor chumps are going to find that I'm very strict about attendance."

It was one o'clock on a sunny afternoon, and the asphalt court at Jefferson Park was shimmering with heat waves. Brian watched as the Bulls shot around before their first practice without Nate and Jim.

Brian couldn't wait to get started. Practice was going to be awesome for the next couple of weeks. No more drilling. No more layup lines. None of that boring stuff.

He was going to make sure the Bulls had *fun*.

"Okay—Chunky Schwartz and Mark Fisher are here," he called out, checking off an imaginary clipboard. "Very good."

Chunky and Mark made up the Bulls' second string. They were decent players—but compared to the rest of the Bulls, they weren't starter quality.

"Go easy on us, Coach," Chunky muttered.

Brian nodded. Chunky always tried as hard as he could—but because of his . . . well, *size*, he usually got tired pretty fast.

 "Uh, you're not going to make us call you 'Coach' or anything, are you, Brian?" Mark asked, adjusting his thick wraparound goggles.

"That's 'Mr. Brian' to you, Mark," Brian replied, secretly wondering how Mark could even see through those goggles. Brian got nervous just looking at them. He held his breath whenever Mark took an outside shot. Mark's shots were usually on target, but he always awkwardly heaved it with both hands over his head.

"Derek Roberts and Jo Meyerson are here," Brian continued. "Very good."

Derek didn't say anything, as usual. He just stood there, tugging on his red, white, and blue wristbands.

"Hey, man, can we get going?" Jo asked. She grabbed a ball and started dribbling behind her back. Brian shook his head. Jo was always mouthing off—just like her brother, Otto. Luckily for the Bulls, though, Jo was as skillful as her brother, but not nearly as sleazy.

"Hold on, now," Brian said. "Let's finish the roll call. Will Hopwood?"

Will nodded at Brian with a bored look on his face.

Brian looked around the playground.

18

"Now where the heck is David Danzig?"

Just then Dave came sprinting through the front gates of Jefferson and onto the court. "Yo, Brian—feed me!" he shrieked.

Brian hurled the ball across the court to him. Dave leapt up, grabbed the pass, and attempted a crazy reverse 360 degree layup. The ball bounced off the backboard with a loud bang.

"All right, Danzig, we'll have none of that during this practice," Brian said in a deep voice. "You're not Michael Jordan. And if there's one thing I can't stand—it's attitude."

Dave bowed his head. "Yes, sir, Mr. White."

Brian grinned. Mr. White was the coach of the Sampton Slashers—Otto's team and the Bulls' archrivals. That *was* just the kind of thing Mr. White would say. He was a total jerk.

"And if you call me Mr. White again, I'll be forced to make you drop and give me twenty," Brian added.

"Uh, can we get started?" Will asked.

"Patience, my man. We're just warming up." Brian clapped his hands. "I'm going to begin with a drill that they once used in the old days."

Brian walked to the free-throw line. He raised the ball over his head with both hands. Suddenly he slammed it down on the court. *Boom!*

The ball bounced high into the air and sailed toward the basket, teetering on the rim for a second before falling in. "The crowd goes crazy!" Brian yelled. He turned to face the rest of the Bulls, who all started clapping and cheering—except Will, who just stood there, frowning.

"Thank you, thank you," Brian said. "Okay, everybody. Line up at the free-throw line. Every one of you make at least one of these old-fashioned free throws."

Everyone ran to get in line. But Will just stood in the middle of the court.

"Don't you think this a waste of time, Brian?" Will asked angrily.

Brian stared at Will. "It'll only take a sec," he said. Will was uptight already, and they'd only just started. Will would chill out after he started having some serious fun, Brian decided.

But after twenty minutes of slamming the ball on the court, only Dave and Derek had actually managed to make the shot.

"Hey, Brian—do you think we can move onto something else?" Jo finally asked. She was beginning to look as fed up as Will.

"Seriously, man," Will added. "We're probably messing up the ball."

"Okay, okay." *Why are Jo and Will getting so bent out of shape?* Brian wondered. Everybody else seemed to be having fun.

"Let's get some three-on-three going here. I'm going to add a little twist. You guys will play half-court, and I'll keep a ten-Mississippi shot clock."

"That's the dumbest thing I ever heard!" Will shouted.

Brian frowned. He'd had enough. Not only was Will taking all the fun out of Brian's practice, he was starting to act like a dork.

"Will, relax. You want me to tell you why it's not dumb? Because it'll force us to pass quickly, shoot from the outside, and crash the boards." Brian counted off three fingers on his right hand. "The three things your brother told us we should work on before he left."

Will glared back at him, but he kept his mouth shut.

"He also told us to have fun, in case you forgot," Brian added.

"Brian, slamming the ball on the court for twenty minutes wasn't what Jim meant by fun," Will shot back. "Believe me."

"Maybe. Maybe not. What do you guys think?" Brian looked around at the rest of the Bulls.

Everyone had become very quiet—the

kind of quiet that happens before a fight.

Brian sighed. "Look Will, I'm going to do things my way while I'm coach, and you can do things your way when you're the coach. And I want to keep a ten-Mississippi shot clock. Anybody else have a problem with that?"

The rest of the team looked up and shook their heads.

"Good," Brian said. "Let's play."

Will had to admit that Brian's idea *was* fun. And it made the Bulls work hard—for a while. But pretty soon Brian started speeding up his shot-clock count, and the game fell apart. Everyone was screaming and laughing and throwing up wild shots—most of which didn't even come close to the basket.

It wasn't a practice anymore. It was a free-for-all.

Finally Will grabbed the ball and held it.

"One-Mississippi, two-Mississippi, three-

Mississippi, four-Mississippi, *ten*!" Brian yelled. "Not quick enough, there, Will."

Mark, Dave, and Chunky started cracking up.

"Brian, this is really, really lame," Will snapped.

The laughter on the court suddenly stopped. There was complete silence, as though someone had clicked off the sound with a remote control.

Brian's eyebrows curved downward. "Says who?"

"Says *me*," Jo cut in. "C'mon, Brian, let's do something else. Everyone's getting tired."

Will looked around. Jo was right—everyone was completely out of breath. Brian's "shot clock" had worn them all out.

Will shook his head. The Bulls had to do *something* today that wasn't a complete waste of time. "I think—" he began.

"Practice is over," Brian shouted, cutting Will off. "Good job, Bulls. Let's all go home and get some rest." He glanced in Will's direction. "I have a feeling we're going to need it for Will's practice tomorrow."

Will felt his face getting hot as the Bulls filed out of Jefferson. He looked at his watch. Brian's practice had only lasted an hour. Usually the Bulls practiced for at least three. *That's it,* Will said to himself. *Tomorrow, the Bulls are going to work.*

CHAPTER 4

Will practiced his foul shots while he waited for the rest of the Bulls to show up at Jefferson. A cool breeze was blowing. Will felt good—primed to practice. It was a perfect day for a long, hard workout.

One by one, the Bulls appeared on the court and began shooting around.

Brian was the last to get there. He was wearing a white T-shirt with the words YOUR MAMA written in big black letters on the front.

"Uh . . . nice shirt, Brian," Will mumbled sarcastically.

Brian just shrugged.

Will spun the ball slowly in his hands. Was Brian mad about what had happened yesterday? Well, he didn't have any reason to be mad—Brian just didn't know how to coach. That's all there was to it.

"All right, let's get started." Will clapped his hands. "I figured we'd loosen up with some suicides."

"Very funny," Dave said, dribbling a ball through his legs.

"It's not supposed to be funny," Will said. "I'm serious."

Dave stopped dribbling. "C'mon, man—suicides? You mean like sprinting up and down the court? Give me a break."

"You heard what Coach Hopwood said," Brian said evenly. "We agreed to let Will coach us. If he wants us to run suicides, we'll run suicides."

"Uh—did I hear you right, Brian?" Dave asked. "Are you going nuts or something?"

"Like I said: Will can do things his way, and I'll do things my way."

For some reason, Will didn't like the sound of that.

The Bulls slowly lined up under the basket. None of them looked very happy. As a matter of fact, they looked downright angry. For a second, Will wondered if he maybe *was* being a little too harsh.

But after all, Nate and Jim made the Bulls run suicides. And good, hard sprinting would keep the team in shape while Nate and Jim were gone.

Will lined up with the rest of them. "On your marks, get set, *go!*" he shouted.

Up and back, up and back, up and back, the Bulls raced across the court. After a couple of minutes, everyone was dripping with sweat and out of breath. And the more they ran, the angrier they looked. Even Will had to admit that suicides were a pain in the butt.

Suddenly Will noticed that Chunky had fallen behind.

Finally Chunky stopped running. "Can't . . . go . . . on," he gasped.

Everyone else stopped, too.

Will was about to tell the rest of the Bulls to keep going—but then he took a closer look at Chunky. Chunky's normally pale skin was bright pink, and he was having a hard time catching his breath. "You all right, man?" Will asked.

"Gotta . . . sit . . . for a sec," Chunky panted.

"That's cool," Will said. "Have a seat on the bench. Everybody else—let's see some hustle!"

"Yo, Will!" a voice shouted behind him. "Do you think we can quit the suicides already? Even Nate and Jim don't make us run *this* long. We don't want anybody dying on us."

Will spun around. *Uh-oh,* he thought. It was Derek. And everyone knew Derek hardly ever opened his mouth unless something was bothering him. *Really* bothering him.

Maybe the Bulls had run enough suicides today.

"Yeah . . . okay," Will said. "Let's take a quick breather. Then we'll get a three-on-three scrimmage going."

The Bulls collapsed on the bench.

Derek glared at Will.

Nobody said a word.

Finally Will nervously broke the silence. "Um . . . I guess we better divide up into teams," he mumbled. "How about Mark, Dave, and me, versus Brian, Derek, and Jo? Chunky, you can rest until you get your breath back. Maybe you can ref for us, too."

As Chunky nodded his thanks, Brian snickered.

"What's so funny?" Will demanded.

Brian's lips curled into a cocky grin. "Those teams are great—if you're in the mood to get whipped."

"We'll see," Will muttered. He knew that Brian was just trying to psych him out—but he wasn't going to have it. The breather was over. He clapped his hands. "Let's go!"

The Bulls slowly divided into the teams Will had called and took to the court.

We'll just see who's going to get whipped, Will said to himself, inbounding the ball to Dave.

When Dave reached the key, Will cut inside. Dave immediately passed the ball to him. But before he had a chance to make a move, Jo and Derek ran to double-team him.

"Hopwood is feeling the pressure," Chunky taunted from the sidelines, imitating a sports announcer.

Will gritted his teeth, trying not to listen. He leaned over and began dribbling slowly, edging toward the basket with his back to Jo and Derek. His plan was to force them back so he could get close enough for an easy layup.

Suddenly a high-pitched whistle pierced the air.

"Three-seconds, Hopwood!" Chunky yelled.

Will rolled his eyes. "Give me a break," he said. He kept dribbling.

Suddenly he realized everyone was staring at him.

"Okay, I promise it'll never happen again. Let's just keep playing."

"Hold on a sec, Will," Brian said. "Why should we give you a break? That was a good call. It's something you gotta watch."

Will couldn't believe his ears. What was Brian trying to pull? This was the guy who was doing "old-fashioned free throws" and making up his own shot clock yesterday!

"Fine!" Will fired the ball at Brian. "Let's play by the rules. We probably need to after our last practice. Your ball."

Will knew he shouldn't get angry. After all, everyone *was* playing seriously. But things weren't quite going the way he had hoped they would. He'd never thought anyone would be counting his time in the lane.

Jo inbounded the ball for Brian's team. Will positioned himself under the basket—keeping his eye on Derek, who was playing the low post to his left.

Brian tossed the ball back to Jo, who rifled it across the court to Derek. Derek took the pass and paused, looking up at the net.

Will figured he was squaring up for a shot. But as Will jumped up to block him, Derek spun off his left foot and drove past Will under the hoop, throwing up a wicked reverse layup with his *left* hand. The ball glanced off the backboard and fell through the net.

Will shook his head. The kid was unbelievable!

"You're the man!" Brian cried, giving Derek a high-five.

"Hopwood gets schooled!" Chunky shouted from the top of the key.

Will turned in Chunky's direction. He'd had just about enough of the play-by-play. "Yo, Chunky, why don't you—"

Suddenly he felt two hands on his hips. The hands tightened around his shorts. And then they yanked.

What the—? Will wondered.

Before Will knew what was happening, his shorts were down by his ankles—and everyone on the court at Jefferson Park was staring at his blue-and-white striped boxers.

Will's mouth fell open. A hot flash of anger shot through him. He snatched up his shorts and spun around.

Standing behind him was Brian, with a big grin on his face. "Y-y-you!" Will sputtered.

Brian shrugged. "I couldn't resist."

Derek and Dave started laughing.

"I'm not sure what the ruling is on this, Brian, but we might have to call you for a technical," Chunky said. He grinned. "Or maybe a flagrant foul—"

"Oh, you think it's funny, huh?" Will pushed Brian hard in the chest and sent him stumbling backward. "How funny would it be if I kicked the crap out of you?"

Brian looked shocked. "Will, what the heck are you—"

"Yo, man, chill!" Derek said, grabbing Will's arm. "He was just kidding around."

Will jerked his arm away from Derek. "Stay out of this!" He kept his eyes glued to Brian. "You got a problem with me or something, Buttface?" he whispered between clenched teeth.

The look on Brian's face quickly turned from surprise to anger.

"Yeah, I do, if you can't take a joke," He shoved Will back with both hands. "And my name's not Buttface, Toilet-breath."

"Hey! Will you guys relax!" Dave yelled. He ran over and stood in between Will and Brian. "Stop acting like dorks. Let's just keep playing, all right?"

"How can we keep playing when Brian keeps messing everything up?" Will snapped.

"C'mon, Will—lighten up, already," Chunky said. "He was joking, man."

"So what if he was?" Jo cut in. "That was a pretty lame thing to do in the middle of the game."

"Who asked *you*?" Brian demanded.

Derek suddenly threw his hands up in the air. "That's it," he said quietly. "I'm leaving."

He turned and walked off the court.

Will just shook his head. "Thanks a lot, Brian," he growled. "Another great practice comes to a close."

Brian stood alone at the free-throw line.

Everyone else had left except Dave. Brian dribbled the ball a few times, then stared at the basket before finally shooting.

The ball hit the back iron and bounced across the court.

Brian bent his head.

"Hey, don't worry about what happened with Will," Dave called as he ran to get the rebound. "He's just really into this coaching thing. Anyway, we don't need the practice." He grinned. "After all, we *are* playing Winsted."

Brian nodded. Dave was right. Anyway, why had Will gotten so uptight? He had just been kidding around. . . .

Just then Dave put up a long shot from the top of the key. It drifted over the court and fell through the net with a *swish*.

SWISH!

Dave held out his hands. "What did I tell you?"

Brian tried to smile, but he couldn't. He had a very bad feeling about the up-coming game.

CHAPTER 5

"What's the good word, Fadeaway?" Nate's dad was standing in front of Bowman's Market, waiting for the Bulls to arrive. "You guys ready?"

Brian shrugged. "I hope so," he muttered.

Mr. Bowman looked at his watch. "Where is everyone? We've got to get going soon." He grinned. "We don't want to

be rude to our hosts in Winsted—at least not before you boys get on the court."

Brian looked around. Nobody else was there yet. In fact, Brian hadn't seen any of the Bulls in three days—not since he had gotten into that fight with Will.

For a second he wondered if anyone was even going to show up at all.

But just then, Chunky walked around the corner—and pretty soon all the Bulls had gathered in front of Bowman's.

Nobody said a word. Nobody even looked at each other. The tension in the air was so thick, Brian felt as though he couldn't breathe.

Brian shot a quick look at Will. Should he try to apologize? But Will was just staring at the ground, looking sour. He didn't look in the mood to talk.

"Everybody ready?" Mr. Bowman asked cheerfully. At least *he* didn't seem to notice that anything was wrong.

The Bulls all crammed into Mr. Bowman's van. Brian ended up getting mashed between Will and Jo in the back seat. *Great,* he thought. *This is going to be loads of fun.*

Mr. Bowman tried to get the Bulls to talk about the game on the ride over to Winsted, but everyone kept quiet.

Just when Brian thought he couldn't stand to be in the crowded van another second, Mr. Bowman pulled up in front of the Winsted Community Center.

"All right, boys—you know what to do," Mr. Bowman said as they headed toward the court. "Have fun, work hard, and beat Winsted."

Brian laughed bitterly. *Have fun, work hard, and beat Winsted.* Nate and Jim had said the exact same thing before they left.

So far, their advice hadn't done the Bulls much good.

"Three . . . two . . . one . . ." chanted the crowd.

Brian dribbled across mid-court, and threw up one last hopeless shot. The ball slammed into the backboard and bounced across the floor.

The gym exploded with cheering.

At the end of the first half, the Wildcats were ahead 24–20.

Brian shook his head. He turned and glanced at Nate's dad. Mr. Bowman was sitting on the bench with his face buried in his hands. Brian quickly looked away. He felt his own face getting red. The first half had been a total humiliation!

The Bulls slowly headed for their locker room. Mr. Bowman followed them in and closed the door behind him.

"All right, listen up," Will said once the door was shut. "We know we should be killing these guys. And we know we're not playing as a team. So let's just forget about what happened last week. We need to talk out there." He slammed his hand on his chair. "If we can't talk to each other, we can't win!"

Brian leaned back in his chair. Will was right. The Bulls had never looked worse on the basketball court. Balls were being thrown away, shots were being missed, and nobody was crashing the boards. The Bulls already had *twelve* turnovers by halftime—more than they usually had in an entire game.

"Too-Tall's right, boys," Mr. Bowman agreed gravely. "Communication is key."

"We also gotta be tough on D," Jo added. "We aren't pressuring them enough."

Will nodded. "That's right. So we're going to switch from a man-to-man to a zone," he went on. "We gotta keep them from getting inside. If we can keep them to the outside and get rebounds, we'll have no problem coming back."

Brian suddenly found himself getting angry. *Why is Will always trying to be the boss?*

"You really think switching to a zone is going to help?" he asked. "They can just stall

all they want against a zone. We just need to tighten up what we've got going so far. A man-to-man will beat a zone any day."

"Oh, it will, huh?" Will asked, his voice rising. "Well maybe, if certain people weren't so lazy on defense."

Brian stood up. "You're calling *me* lazy? You're—"

"Let's just take it easy, guys," Mr. Bowman interrupted gently but firmly. "There's no reason to raise your voice. We all know what we need to do out there."

Dave laughed, then shook his head. "If we knew that, we wouldn't be losing to the worst team in the league."

"We'd be winning if anyone was playing half-decently," Will snapped. He put his hand on the door, then turned around and pointed his finger at Brian. "We'll stick with a man-to-man, if that's what you want. But you better start hustling."

Will cut across the court into the center of the lane. Dave fired the ball at him. With his back to his defender, he dribbled once, then spun and put up a short jumper.

SWOOSH!

Will brushed the sweat off his forehead as he ran back on D. With three minutes left in the third quarter, the Bulls had finally managed to tie the game, 32–32. But it had been a nasty struggle. Will knew the Bulls still hadn't gotten into a rhythm yet. Most of their points had been lucky, and the Wildcats had blown a bunch of easy shots.

The Wildcats took the ball quickly downcourt. They began working the ball around the perimeter, looking for a way to pass inside. Will could tell that they were mad—and nervous—about having blown their lead. He kept alert, covering the Wildcats' center tightly.

But as the ball was being whipped around, Will noticed that Brian was several feet away from his man—a short kid with frizzy black hair. The kid was open for a possible outside shot in the left corner.

"Brian, play tighter," Will called.

Suddenly the ball was passed to the frizzy-haired kid.

"Tighter!" Will shouted.

As Brian ran over, the kid faked a shot. Brian leapt into the air, giving the kid enough time to dribble around him and penetrate inside for an easy layup.

"Winsted thirty-four, Branford thirty-two," the scorekeeper announced.

"Way to go, Brian," Will muttered.

Brian jerked his head around as Dave took the ball downcourt. "Shut up, Will. I was doing fine until you opened your big mouth."

Will knew he shouldn't have said anything. But how could Brian blame *him* for getting burned?

"De-fense, De-fense, De-fense," chanted the crowd as the Bulls crossed the half-court line.

Dave took the ball upcourt and dished the ball to Brian when he reached the top of the key. Will headed inside the lane, posting up on the Wildcats' center. The kid was a couple of inches shorter than Will, and Will knew he could outjump him for an easy shot.

Will raised his arms—but Brian passed the ball across the court to Derek. After pausing for a second, Derek threw the ball back to Dave.

"Yo, you guys!" Will began waving his arms wildly, pushing toward the basket. "I'm open—"

Screeeech! The sound of a whistle filled the gym.

"Three-second violation, Bulls," called the ref. "Wildcats' ball."

The crowd started cheering again.

Will stomped his foot on the floor.

Three seconds! How could he have let that happen?

Brian shook his head. "You gotta watch for that, man."

"Mind your own business," Will mumbled.

"It is my business if we lose because of your dumb mistakes," Brian said.

"Well maybe if you had actually looked *inside,* you would have seen that I was open, idiot."

Suddenly Brian shoved him hard— and Will went sprawling on the floor.

Everyone in the gym gasped.

The ref's whistle fell out of his mouth. "All right, all right, let's take a little time out," he said sternly. "Take it easy, boys. I won't have any fighting on my court."

He reached out his hand and hoisted Will to his feet. "You all right, son?" he asked.

Will nodded. He was too shocked to speak.

Brian ducked his head and turned away.

Will walked to the Bulls' bench in a

daze. He noticed that the Wildcats were all staring at Brian. Then he realized it was probably the first time they had ever seen a fight break out between members of the same team.

Come to think of it, Will had never seen teammates fight each other during a game, either.

He sat down on the bench next to Mark, who looked at him with wide eyes. "I can't believe Brian would do that," Mark whispered.

Will nodded grimly. He decided right then and there to sit the fourth quarter out. If Brian wanted to keep playing, fine. But Will wasn't going to play with him. Brian had gone too far.

In fact, Will didn't want to play with Brian again.

Ever.

CHAPTER 6

"Yes!" Dave cried. "I've already scored fifty points!"

Brian sat on the rug in the middle of Dave's living room, staring glumly at the TV screen. Rain pounded against the windows.

Dave sat next to him, feverishly wrestling with his control pad as he played *NBA Jam*.

"Too bad you couldn't score fifty points against Winsted," Brian muttered.

Dave brushed his blond bangs out of his face with his free hand and grimaced.

"Hey, man, maybe yesterday's game will teach us a lesson."

"Like what?" Brian shook his head. "That the Branford Bulls should give up basketball and join the local computer club? Dave, we got whipped by the worst team in the League."

A few seconds later, the TV screen flashed GAME OVER.

Dave sighed and put down his control pad. "No, Brian. It should teach us that if we get into stupid fights for no reason at all, we'll lose."

Brian shot an angry look at Dave. "Hey—what happened yesterday wasn't my fault. If Will hadn't tried to be the boss, everything would have been fine."

"No, Brian—"

Just then the doorbell rang.

Dave hopped off the floor. "Hey, what do you know? Someone's at the door. I'll get it." He dashed out of the room.

Hmm, Brian thought suspiciously. Dave sounded funny. And he hadn't mentioned that he had invited anyone else over. Suddenly Brian began to get a sick feeling in his stomach. "Dave," he called. "Please tell me you didn't invite Will over. . . ." His voice trailed off and his eyes narrowed when he saw who Dave was leading into the living room.

Dave *had* invited Will over.

Will glared down at Brian from where he stood in the entrance to the living room. He jerked a finger in Brian's direction and turned to face Dave angrily. "What's *he* doing here?"

"What am *I* doing here?" Brian snapped. "For your information—"

"Yo!" Dave interrupted. "Everyone chill. For *your* information, I invited both of you here. I figured since it's raining and we aren't having practice, now's the perfect time to end this dumb fight once and for all."

"Fine." Will shrugged. "I know the perfect way to end it. Kick Brian off the team."

Brian's mouth fell open. He knew Will was mad at him—*really* mad—but he never would have imagined in a million years that Will would want him off the Branford Bulls.

"You're serious," Brian whispered.

"Dead serious," Will replied.

"Will, man, you're just mad right now," Dave put in quickly. "You're not thinking straight."

"Oh yeah?" Will shot back. "I called Mark and Jo this morning. They think I'm right, too."

Brian swallowed. Mark and Jo wanted him off the team, too? A cold sweat broke out on the back of his neck. Was this really happening?

"Well, what about Derek and Chunky?" Brian asked in a shaky voice. "*They* don't want me off the team."

Will hesitated. "Chunky doesn't," he said finally. "Derek doesn't want to pick sides."

"What about you, Dave?" Brian demanded. "Do you want me off the team, too?"

Dave looked at Will, then at Brian, then at Will again. "I don't want to pick sides, either," he said. "That's why I invited you over here. I thought we could work this out. . . ."

Brian couldn't believe it. *Dave* wasn't even sticking up for him. "Thanks for backing me up, man," he said angrily. "Well, it was nice knowing you, pal." He stood up. "Maybe I'll go play for the Slashers."

"Hold up a sec," Will said, raising his hands. He took a deep breath. "I've got an idea. We can settle this on the court."

Brian raised his eyebrows. "What are you getting at?"

"Either you go or I go. So I say we play a game—three-on-three—to decide. The loser leaves the team."

"A grudge match?" Brian ran his fingers over his short fade haircut and thought for a moment. Maybe Will had a good idea. Right now, humiliating Will Hopwood on the basketball court sounded like the perfect solution to his problems.

And then he'd never have to play with Will again.

Brian nodded. "You got it."

"You sure you guys want to do this?" Dave asked, his voice quavering. "I mean this sounds sort of drastic. . . ."

"I'm sure," Brian said. "I'll tell you what, Dave—you can ref." His voice hardened. "That way you don't have to pick sides."

"Good idea," Will put in before Dave could reply. "Then it's settled. Three days from now at Jefferson. One o'clock."

Always trying to be the boss, Brian thought.

He looked Will in the eye. "I'll be there."

CHAPTER 7

Brian stood at the half-court line, waiting to check the ball.

"All right, everyone, you know the rules," Dave called. "Half-court, first team to twenty, win by two, losers take the ball out."

Brian licked his lips.

"We know the rules, Dave," Will said in a dull voice. "Let's get started. I want to get this over with as quickly as possible."

The day of the grudge match was hot, cloudy, and humid. The air at Jefferson felt like pea soup. Brian had already begun to sweat, and the game hadn't even started yet.

But as he took the ball downcourt, Brian realized that he wasn't sweating just because of the weather. He was nervous. At least Derek was on his team. But so was Chunky, who would probably get tired—and would probably do more harm than good.

Will, on the other hand, was playing with Jo and Mark.

Brian didn't think the teams were fair. But what could he do about it? He knew he had to make the best of it. He *had* to win.

Brian dribbled for a few seconds at the top of the key, then hurled the ball to Derek, who was playing the high post on the left side of the lane. Derek immediately spotted up and banked a flawless jump shot off the backboard.

"Yes!" Brian cried. He slapped Derek's hand as they positioned themselves on defense. "I'm going to need a lot of those today, man."

Derek nodded. "Don't worry. I schooled

Will before—and you can bet I'll school him again."

Mark tossed the ball to Brian, who checked it at the top of the key. Brian knew that the toughest part of playing D would be keeping Mark and Jo from getting the ball inside to Will. Will played his best right under the hoop.

Mark fired the ball at Jo, who was standing near the sideline on the right side of the court. Brian ran to cover her, but she pump-faked once, breezing past him. He turned just in time to see Will setting a pick on Derek, preventing him from getting to her. Jo dashed into the lane for an easy layup.

"Hey Brian," Will yelled. "Maybe you should borrow Mark's goggles. You don't seem to be seeing the court too well."

Brian struggled to ignore Will's trash talk. If he got angry, he would only play worse.

"C'mon, let's go," he called as he gave

the ball to Jo to check. "Let's make things happen out here."

As he dribbled near the free-throw line, he saw that Will and Mark were double-teaming Derek. Jo was covering him—and Chunky was wide open.

Brian hesitated for a second. Should he pass to Chunky? There was no telling what he would do with the ball—

Whap!

Suddenly the ball went flying out of Brian's hands and over his head. Jo had slapped it away from him. And by the time Brian was able to react, she had already turned and beaten him to the basket for another layup.

"Yo, Brian, maybe you should just quit while you're ahead," Will called, smirking. "Getting burned twice in the first two minutes must hurt."

"Not as much as getting your face punched in," Brian shot back. "Now shut up and let me play."

Will's face darkened. "What did you say, you little—"

"Stop it!" Jo shouted. "We came here to

play hoops. If you fools want to fight, go ahead. Then the rest of us can go home."

"Absolutely," Dave added. "If you two just want to fight, I don't see why you need me here as ref at all."

"No, no, you're right," Will said, backing off. He looked at Brian. "I want to make sure we finish this game."

Brian took a quick second to catch his breath before he checked the ball in to Jo. He felt as if he were about to explode. *Just chill,* he told himself. *You've been dissed, but now it's time you settle the score.*

Jo ran up to pressure Brian the moment the ball was in play. Instead of protecting the ball, Brian turned to face her, figuring she would go for another steal. Sure enough, she swatted—and he dribbled once between his legs, spun, and whipped right past her.

"Nice!" Derek yelled as Brian flew across the free-throw line.

But Will stood squarely in the lane, blocking his path to the hoop. Brian slowed and turned around, keeping his back to the basket. He edged a little closer, then bobbed his head once. It was just enough to bring Will to his toes—giving Brian the split second he needed to outjump him.

Brian pushed off with his feet and spun. His fadeaway jumper barely cleared the top of Will's fingertips.

"Now who's getting burned?" he whispered under his breath.

Faking Will out had felt good. But the game was still only tied at two baskets each. The grudge match had barely started.

Brian wiped his forehead. It was going to be a *long* afternoon.

CHAPTER 8

Will watched as Jo fired a jump shot from the left of the key. The ball sailed over his head and fell through the hoop.

"Sweet," Will managed between breaths. "Seventeen-fourteen."

Will felt as if he were about to pass out. The court had never been this hot and sticky. It was already almost two o'clock, and the grudge match was still far from over.

But the longer the Bulls played against each other, the more Will wanted to win.

Everyone else looked like they just wanted to go home.

Dave had already left. He had stormed off the court a few minutes ago without saying a word.

Will hadn't been surprised. After all, Dave hadn't wanted to pick sides, and grudge matches weren't pretty to watch. As a matter of fact, they usually got pretty ugly. And this one was no exception.

"C'mon!" Will shouted. "Three more baskets. Let's go!"

Brian was dribbling the ball at the top of the key. Will was sure he was either going to shoot or pass to Derek. That's what Brian had been doing all afternoon.

Will couldn't blame him. Chunky was exhausted. He could barely move, much less dribble or shoot.

Suddenly Brian cut inside, heading straight for Will. As Will put his hands up to block him, Brian leapt into the air, swinging his arms down for a scoop shot. Will saw the move and tried to stuff him—but ended up hacking Brian's arms just as the ball left his hands.

"Foul!" Brian yelled. "And if this were the NBA, it would be a flagrant. What's the matter, Will? Can't stop me clean, so you got to play dirty?"

"You make a call every time someone breathes on you," Will shouted back. "You want to call that little tap a foul, fine. Just stop your whining and take the ball out." Will knew he had fouled Brian—but he was way too angry to admit that right now.

Brian glared at Will as he pointed the ball over to Jo for a check. Then he fired it in to Derek, who quickly returned it to him for a baseline jumper.

"Seventeen-fifteen," Brian shouted, raising his arms over his head. "The opera ain't over till the fat lady sings!"

Will grabbed the ball and slapped it hard once before tossing it to Jo. "C'mon, guys. Let's get it together."

Jo checked the ball

quickly and passed it off to Mark, who slowed it down near the left side of the key. Mark peered at the basket through his glasses.

Oh, no, Will thought grimly. Mark was going to try one of his famous over-the-head shots. He usually sank them, but right now he was too far away. Will instantly cut into the lane, trying to get open for a pass. But as soon as he was in the paint, Derek ran to cover him, putting himself between Will and the basket.

Will pushed his back hard against Derek, forcing him to edge closer and closer to the hoop . . .

Just then, he heard someone counting.

" . . . two Mississippi, three Mississippi—"

It was Brian!

"Three seconds!" Brian shouted, pointing his finger at Will. "Our ball!"

Will felt like screaming. "You're actually going to try to pull that crap? You're *that* cheap?"

"Nothing cheap about it," Brian said calmly. "Rules are rules, man. Learn to play by 'em."

"You're just scared you're going to lose," Will shot back.

"And *you've* sunk so low that you gotta cheat to win," Brian growled.

"I've got to cheat?" Will's voice rose. "You're calling me a cheater? I'm going to—"

All of a sudden Will felt a large hand on his shoulder.

"What the heck is going on here?" demanded a deep voice.

Uh-oh, Will thought, his stomach sinking. The voice was *very* familiar. But it couldn't be. . . .

Will spun around.

It *was*.

Standing behind him was his brother, Jim.

And standing right next to him was Nate.

Will swallowed.

Nate and Jim looked more angry than Will had thought was possible. Their faces were both twisted and trembling with rage. *Angry* wasn't even the right word.

They were *furious*.

"You heard me," Jim said, keeping his

hand on Will's shoulder. "What the heck is going on here?"

Will opened his mouth, but nothing came out.

"Well?" Jim spat.

Finally Will thought of something to say. "Uh . . . aren't you guys supposed to be at basketball camp?"

Nate laughed once—a short, harsh laugh. "Yeah, as a matter of fact we are. And we were having the time of our lives, hanging with NBA greats, getting tips from the pros. But you see, Will, I got this call from my dad a couple of days ago. He said you guys had gone completely nuts."

Will felt blood rush into his face. "He did?"

"Yup. And even worse, he said you lost to the Wildcats. He told me I better come home before you killed each other."

"Y-you guys came home early?" Will stammered.

"That's right," Jim said. "We also happened to run into Dave at Bowman's a couple of minutes ago. And *he* told us some crazy story about you and Brian getting into a fight. He said you were playing a grudge match to decide who should be kicked off the team."

Will began to feel sick.

Nate bent down and looked Will in the eye. "And I said, 'No, Dave, I don't believe you. That's just *too* crazy.'"

Jim tightened his grip on Will's shoulder. His eyes were blazing. "So Dave told us to come down and see for ourselves," he whispered between clenched teeth.

Will's eyes darted from Nate to Jim, then back to Nate again.

"I-I-I . . ." he stuttered.

"This game is over!" Jim bellowed, finally letting Will go. "I don't know *what* happened while we were gone, and to be honest, I really don't care. But I want every single one of you off this court *now*."

All the Bulls were frozen, staring at their coaches.

"Did you hear me?" Jim demanded. "I said *now*!"

With that, the Bulls turned and ran.

Will heard Jim's voice ringing out of the playground as he dashed through the front gates and bolted down the street.

"And don't bother coming back until you can act like normal, civilized human beings. Until then, every member of the Branford Bulls is suspended!"

Will peered inside the front gates of Jefferson. *Whew*, he thought. *The court's empty.*

It was another beautiful, sunny day in Branford. A perfect day for hoops. But Will didn't feel like playing with anyone. After what had happened yesterday, he just wanted to be alone.

Will began shooting around at the far end of the court. As far as he was concerned, he could play alone for the rest of his life. He wasn't going to say he was sorry until Brian said *he* was sorry. After all, it was all Brian's fault.

Wasn't it?

Suddenly Will heard another ball bouncing on the cement.

He looked over his shoulder.

Oh, no, Will thought, clenching his teeth. *It's Brian.*

Brian shot a blank glance at Will, then stomped over to the other end of the court.

Fine, Will thought. If Brian wanted to shoot around at Jefferson, no problem. It was a free country.

Will decided to work on his free throws. That way he wouldn't have to look in Brian's direction.

He positioned himself at the line and dribbled the ball hard a few times, staring at the basket. He felt his face getting hot. *C'mon, man,* he told himself. *Concentrate.* Finally, he brought the ball up. He took a deep breath. The ball floated over the court. . . .

Slam! Just as the shot reached the hoop, another ball came flying out of nowhere. It struck Will's ball and sent it hurtling away from the basket.

"Whoops! Sorry, dude," a voice snickered. "Guess I just didn't time my shot right.

Will spun around. A stocky kid with a greasy crew cut and a round, mean-looking face was grinning at him.

"Otto!" Will shouted. "What the heck are *you* doing here?"

"What's it look like, dummy?" he replied. "Shooting around."

Will's jaw tightened. "Why don't you go shoot around in Sampton, where you belong? We don't want you here."

Otto wrinkled his face into a sad puppy look. "Oh, no. The Branford Buttheads don't want me here. That really hurts my feelings." He picked up Will's ball and put up a shot.

"I'm serious, man," Will said. "Get out of here."

"For your information, Hopwood, anyone can play on this lousy playground," Otto stated. "And that's what we're going to do."

Will's brow furrowed. "We?"

Just then a tall, pale kid with a black

71

wool hat and a short kid with a mop of red hair slunk through the front gate.

"Yo, Spider! Matt!" Otto called. "Over here!"

Will put his hands on his forehead. He couldn't believe it. The Sampton Slashers had come to Jefferson! But why? Just when he thought things couldn't get any worse. . . .

Spider took a look at Will, then glanced downcourt at Brian. "Beat it, cheeseball," he said to Will. He jerked a thumb in Brian's direction. "In case you didn't notice, the Branford Buttheads are practicing down there."

"I'm not going anywhere," Will snapped. "I was here first. You guys go shoot around at the other end." He grabbed Otto's ball and drove to the basket for a layup.

"But we can't, Hopwood," Otto called. "Unless you tell your lame friend to quit hogging the court."

"Tell him yourself," Will muttered.

"Hey lamebrain!" Otto shouted. "Hopwood here wants you to quit hogging the court!"

Will's stomach twisted. He looked in Brian's direction. Brian put up a jump shot, then turned his head as the ball fell through the hoop. "I don't give a crap what Hopwood wants!" he shouted back.

Otto's eyes opened wide. Then he started giggling. "Wow, did you hear that, Hopwood? You just going to sit back and take that?"

Will opened his mouth, but nothing came out.

"Well?" Otto demanded. "What are you, some kind of wuss?"

Spider grinned. "Hey, lame-o!" he called toward Brian. "Hopwood says your mama smells funny!"

Will held his breath, but Brian didn't say anything. He just kept shooting.

"Man, this is sad." Otto doubled over with laughter. "You guys are the biggest bunch of wimps I've ever seen. C'mon, why don't you go down there and kick his butt?"

Will was silent.

"Yo, I got an idea," Spider said suddenly. His thin lips curved into a smile. "How about a little three-on-two, Hopwood? The Bulls versus the Slashers. Right here, right now."

Will licked his lips.

"What are you, chicken?" Spider began flapping his arms. *"Brawk! Brawk!"*

Otto and Matt quickly joined in. *"Brawk! Brawk!"* they all shouted together.

Finally Will exploded. "Three-on-two against you morons! You got it!" He cupped his hands to his mouth. "Brian, these dopes actually think they can beat us in a game of three-on-two. What do you say we show 'em what's up?"

Brian stopped shooting. He glared at Will. "Some other time."

"Brawk! Brawk! Brawk!" shouted Otto, Spider, and Matt, flapping their arms like chicken wings.

Brian shook his head and sneered. "Do you guys have any idea how stupid you look?"

The Slashers stopped squawking. "Well, are you going to play or not?" Otto yelled.

"You really want to get beaten that

badly? Fine!" Brian picked up his ball and walked upcourt. "It's on."

For a second, Will forgot how mad he was at Brian. Right now he just wanted to crush the Slashers. No, not crush. *Destroy.*

"First team to twenty, win by two, losers—"

"Well, what have we here?" asked a girl's voice.

Will turned around. His heart soared. It was Jo!

"Get out of here, Jo," Otto told his sister. "No girls allowed."

Jo folded her arms across her chest. "You're just scared I'm going to cream you, like I always do at home." A slow grin curled on her face. "Three-on-two, huh? That doesn't seem fair, Otto. Let's even things up a little bit."

"That's what I like to hear," Will said, giving Jo a low five. "You ready for some action?"

Jo nodded. She looked at Brian, then at Will again. Then she laughed. "Action? That's what I came for." She sneered at Otto. "It runs in the family."

"Fine," Otto said sharply. "Figures you wimps had to have someone bail you out."

Otto spoke tough, but Will noticed that he didn't look nearly as psyched as he did before. In fact, Otto looked nervous. Will smiled. *This is going to be fun,* he thought.

"Let's go, Bulls!" Brian shouted.

Brian took the pass from Jo and dribbled the ball to the left of the lane. Spider ran to cover him. But just as Spider reached him, Brian faked, spun, and drove toward the hoop—leaving Spider in the dust. He banked in an easy layup.

"Nice!" Jo shouted. "Seventeen-twelve. You suckers want to give up yet?"

"Shut up, dweeb," Otto snapped. He began dribbling the ball toward the hoop.

Brian laughed as he got set on defense. He was surprised how much fun he was having—even if he was playing with Will. They hadn't said a word to each other for the past forty-five minutes. As long as they both kept their mouths shut, they could get along great.

And of course, beating the Slashers *always* felt good.

"Let's get this over with," Otto muttered. He looked around from the top of the key. "I want to get out of this dump as soon as possible."

Otto protected the ball with his back as Jo came out to guard him. Suddenly Otto jerked his head forward, then hesitated before taking off down the lane. His move was enough to get one step ahead of Jo.

Brian watched as Otto bolted toward the basket. Will was standing directly under the net. As Otto went up for the layup, Will leapt forward with perfect timing—and slammed his hand down on the ball just as Otto released it.

"Yes!" Brian shouted.

Jo recovered the ball and brought it

back out. She dribbled behind her back twice before swishing a beauty—lots of arc, perfect rotation.

"Man, you guys are just like Thanksgiving turkey," Jo hooted at Otto. "You keep getting stuffed."

"Oh yeah? Well . . . well, you got nothing,'" Otto stammered. "Now shut up."

"Great comeback, Otto," Will said sarcastically. "You talk trash almost as well as you play hoops. You stink at both."

Otto stared at Will before checking the ball with Jo. "At least I don't look like some overgrown beanpole."

Will shook his head. "I'm not even going to answer that."

Everyone fell silent as Otto dribbled the ball into the right corner.

Brian wiped his forehead and narrowed his eyes. Otto needed to be schooled in a major way. He glanced at Otto's long, black shorts. Then he smiled.

He knew just what to do.

Otto passed the ball to Matt when he reached the top of the key. Brian kept his eyes glued on Otto as Otto ran around the perimeter, looking for a way to get open inside.

All of a sudden, Otto dashed into the lane. Spider fired the ball at him. Otto spun and squared up for a shot. But just as he was lifting the ball, Brian snuck behind him, grabbed onto his shorts— and yanked as hard as he could.

The shot fell three feet short of the basket.

Everyone on the court gasped.

Brian blinked. He couldn't believe it. Otto was wearing the most stupid underwear he had ever seen.

Otto's underwear was bright green, with little pink pigs printed all over it.

Otto froze for a second. His face turned bright red. Then he bent over and slowly pulled up his shorts.

Brian shot a look at Will.

Will's mouth slowly turned up in a grin.

Brian smiled.

Then Will chuckled.

Before Brian knew it, he and Will were rolling around on the court, shrieking with laughter.

"Nice briefs, Otto," Brian finally managed. "Your mommy get you those?"

"She did!" Jo exclaimed gleefully. "He's had those since he was six years old!"

"You guys just wait!" Otto shouted. "Come game time, we're going to cream you!"

Then he turned and ran out of the park.

Spider and Matt looked at each other, then chased after him.

"Wait up guys!" Will yelled. "Don't you want to finish the game? Hey, Otto, I kinda like those little pigs. . . ."

Brian and Will stood up. Brian turned to Will, then raised his hand high over his head. Will did the same. After pausing a second, they both swung their hands around, meeting for a loud, solid low five.

Slap!

"Nothing like teamwork," Brian said. "Know what I'm saying?"

Will and Brian sat on the bench outside Bowman's. The late afternoon sun felt hot on Will's face. He glanced at

Brian. Both of them were fidgeting. Nate and Jim loomed over them, their faces stern, their arms crossed.

"So you guys are really trying to tell us that you're ready to play again?" Nate demanded. "After that ridiculous stunt you pulled?"

Will and Brian nodded silently.

Nate shook his head. "Well, what makes you think we'll believe you?"

Will gulped.

"Yeah, how are we supposed be sure?" Jim asked. He leaned forward. "Prove it."

Neither Will nor Brian said a word.

Jim raised his eyebrows. "We're waiting."

Finally Will cleared his throat. "Um . . . I really don't know what to say." He looked at the ground. "I mean, besides that I'm sorry. It was pretty much all my fault. I was way too bossy and everything—"

"No, it wasn't all Will's fault," Brian interrupted. "I mean, I was horsing around the whole time. It was my fault, too."

Will looked up. Both Nate and Jim were grinning.

"What?" he asked.

Nate sighed. "I'll tell you what, boys. We'll give you guys one last shot. But on one condition. You guys play as a team. Got it?"

Will nodded.

"And if you ever, ever try anything as stupid as a grudge match again, the two of you can consider yourselves off the Branford Bulls," Jim said.

Brian looked up. "We understand."

Nate and Jim turned and began walking down the street.

Will's eyes met Brian's across the bench.

The two of them smiled.

"The Bulls are back!" Will yelled, leaping off the bench.

Brian jumped up to stand next to him.

"Show time!" they shouted together.

CHAPTER 10

Will tensed his legs for the jump. The ref stuck the ball between Will and the opposing center, then tossed it high into the air.

Will leapt up and swatted the ball to Brian. Dave was already halfway to the basket. Brian turned and whipped the ball to Dave, who took it all the way home for the layup.

NOTHING BUT NET

"All right!" Will shouted.

"Branford two, Portsmouth zero," the scorekeeper announced.

"Nice!" Nate called from the sidelines.

Will slapped Brian's hand as they ran back on D.

A week had passed since Will and Brian had managed to convince Nate and Jim that the Bulls were ready to play as a team again. And during that week, Nate and Jim had worked the Bulls harder then they had ever worked them before.

But Will hadn't minded. The Bulls needed it for today's game. The Portsmouth Panthers were one of the best teams in the league.

Somehow, Nate and Jim had also managed to make practices a lot of fun. Instead of suicides, they'd had the Bulls run relay races with candy bars—"Winner eats all." Will grinned. After all, practice should never be *too* serious.

"C'mon, Bulls," Jim called. "Let's see some tough D."

The Panthers' guard stopped when he reached the top of the key. Dave covered him tightly, but the guard was able to get the ball inside to the Panthers' center.

The center was a big kid with buckteeth. Will tried to keep him from getting close to the basket, but it was hard. The kid was almost as tall as he was. He backed into Will, then spun around for a quick two points.

"Let's go, Portsmouth, let's go," chanted the crowd.

Jo quickly inbounded the ball to Dave. Will sprinted downcourt. He rushed into the lane as Dave slowed the pace across mid-court.

Dave dished the ball back off to Jo at the free-throw line. She hurled it to Brian, who was standing on the baseline near the left corner.

Will was posting up on the kid with the buckteeth. He was facing Brian, open for a pass on the inside. Suddenly he noticed Brian was flashing three fingers at him with his left hand while he dribbled with his right.

Three seconds! Will bolted out of the lane just as Brian released a jump shot.

"Nice!" Will shouted, breathing a sigh of relief.

"Nothing to it." Brian flashed Will a grin.

"Branford four, Portsmouth two," announced the score-keeper.

By the end of the first quarter, the Bulls were up 10–6.

"Nice work out there, guys," said Jim before the Bulls went back on-court. "We just gotta watch for the inside pass. Their center is good. Derek, if you see the pass coming, double-team the guy with Will."

Derek nodded.

"All right, team—show 'em what you've got!" Nate cried.

The Bulls ran back out oncourt for the second quarter. Will was psyched. Now was the time to make up for the game in Winsted. It was time to show the Danville County League who was boss.

Dave brought the ball downcourt for the Bulls. Will headed for the lane, then paused at the left of the foul line. Dave fired the ball to Derek on the right side of the court. As Derek caught Dave's pass, Will met Derek's eyes and jerked his head toward the basket.

Derek flashed a rare grin.

Suddenly Will threw himself into the lane and leapt toward the hoop. Derek lobbed the ball into the air, hitting Will at the peak of his jump. Will caught it and let it bounce off his fingertips. The ball plopped into the net.

"Alley-oop!" shouted Chunky from the sidelines. "What a move!"

Will laughed. "Awesome pass!" he yelled at Derek.

"Awesome shot!" Derek yelled back.

"Now that's what I like to see," Nate called. "Teamwork! Keep it up!"

The Panthers' guard whipped the ball inside to the kid with buckteeth. Derek dashed into the lane. As the kid went up for a shot, Derek dived forward and swatted the ball out of his hands.

Will recovered the ball and launched it to Jo, who beat the rest of the Panthers downcourt for a layup.

The ref blew his whistle. "Time out Portsmouth," he called.

Will glanced at the scoreboard as he trotted toward the bench. With thirty seconds left in the game, the Bulls were up by a basket, 38–36.

"All right guys, the Panthers are going to be desperate," Nate said into the huddle. "They're going to try to foul us if we get the ball back. Let's use that to our advantage." He grinned. "It's time to play Slasher-style basketball. Any chance you get, take the ball to the hoop. That way we can draw the foul *and* maybe get a three-point play out of it."

Jim looked around the huddle at all the Bulls until he got to Will and Brian, who were standing next to each other. "You two think you can manage to behave yourselves for the last few seconds?"

"I don't know, Coach," Will said. He flashed a lopsided grin at Brian. "We'll try."

"As long as Will isn't wearing underwear with pink pigs on it, I think we can get along fine," Brian said.

Nate wrinkled his eyebrows. "Fadeaway, man, you are one weird kid."

Brian shrugged. "Not as weird as *some* kids we know."

Will turned his attention to the game. The Bulls had switched to a zone defense. The Panthers whipped the ball around the outside, looking for an inside pass. But it was no use. The seconds ticked off the clock.

Suddenly Dave hopped forward and intercepted a bounce pass between the Panthers' guards. He sprinted downcourt. One of the guards chased after him. Just as Dave went for the layup, the other kid hacked his arms.

The sound of the ref's whistle echoed through the gym as the ball spun around the rim. Finally it fell in.

"And the basket counts!" Will shouted.

Dave stood at the free-throw line. He spun the ball once in his hands, then put it up.

"Branford forty-one, Portsmouth thirty-six," the scorekeeper announced.

Chunky and Mark began counting down with the clock as the Panthers took the ball up-court for the last time.

"*Eight . . . seven . . .*"

The Panthers desperately looked for a shot.

"*Six . . . five . . . four . . .*"

Finally the kid with the buckteeth grabbed the ball and put it up from deep outside. It landed right in Brian's arms.

"*Three . . . two . . . one!*" Chunky, Mark, Nate, and Jim all jumped off the bench at the same time.

"Way to go, Bulls!" Nate shouted.

"Nice work!" Jim yelled.

"The Panthers get punished," Brian added.

Will smiled.

Trash talk had never sounded sweeter.

About the Author

Hank Herman is a writer and newspaper columnist who lives in Connecticut with his wife, Carol, and their three sons, Matt, Greg, and Robby.

His column, The Home Team, appears in the *Westport News*. It's about kids, sports, and life in the suburbs.

Although Mr. Herman was formerly the editor-in-chief of *Health* magazine, he now writes mostly about sports. At one time, he was a tennis teacher, and he has also run the New York City Marathon. He coaches kids' basketball every winter and Little League baseball every spring.

He runs, bicycles, skis, kayaks, and plays tennis and basketball on a regular basis. Mr. Herman admits that he probably spends about as much time playing, coaching, and following sports as he does writing.

Of all sports, basketball is his favorite.